CHAPTER ONE

The Old pirate at the "Admiral Benbow"

My name is Jim Hawkins and I'm going to tell you the story of Treasure Island. It began when I was a boy. My father had an inn by the sea called the "Admiral Benbow". One day an old seaman arrived with a big sea-chest. He was tall and strong.

'Bring me a glass of rum!' he said to my father. 'Are there many people here?'

My father said no.

'Good! I'll stay here. You can call me captain. Take my chest up to my room.'

Every day he went to the cliffs and looked at the sea with his telescope. And every day he asked us: 'Do you sometimes notice any seamen here?' We began to understand that he didn't want to meet any seamen. One day he said to me, 'Tell me when you see a seaman with one leg, and I'll give you some money.'

Sometimes the old captain drank a lot of rum. Then he sang and he told us some horrible stories. He didn't pay us any money, so my poor father was unhappy and he became ill. One afternoon Dr Livesey came to see him. In the evening the doctor smoked his pipe with some friends. The old captain was there.

'Silence!' he said. 'I'm going to tell you a story.'

'Are you talking to me, sir?' said Dr Livesey angrily.

'Yes!'

'You drink too much rum, sir,' said the doctor. 'One day you will die.'

The angry captain took a knife from his pocket.

'Put that knife back in your pocket,' the doctor said calmly, 'or you will be arrested. I am also a magistrate.'

The captain put the knife in his pocket and sat down. He was very quiet that evening.

That winter was cold and my father became worse. One morning in January a seaman arrived.

'Is there a man called Bill here?' he asked.

I said there was only the captain and he was on the beach. Then the man waited behind the door, so when the captain came in, he didn't see him.

'Bill!'

The captain looked round quickly. His face was white.

'You know me, Bill,' the man said. 'We're old friends.'

'Black Dog!'

'Yes! I've come to see you.'

'What do you want?'

They sat at the table with some rum. The door was open and Black Dog sat near it. I couldn't hear their conversation. Then there was a lot of noise and the table and chairs fell over. I saw Black Dog with blood on his shoulder. Then he ran out of the door. The captain's cutlass had blood on it.

'Bring me some rum, Jim!' he said.

When I came back with the rum, the captain was on the floor. His eyes were closed and his face was very white.

Then Dr Livesey arrived to see my father. He looked at the captain and said, 'He drinks too much rum and so he's ill.' Then he showed me a tattoo on the captain's arm.

'Look, his name is written here,' he said. 'Billy Bones.'

After a few moments the captain opened his eyes.

'Now, Mr Bones, don't drink rum again or you'll die,' the doctor told him.

We took him upstairs to his room and put him in his bed. At twelve o'clock I went into his room with some medicine. But he said that he wanted a glass of rum.

'But the doctor I began.

'Oh, the doctor! What does he know about me? Bring me one glass of rum, Jim, and I'll give you some money.'

'I don't want your money,' I said. But I brought the rum.

'How long must I stay in bed, Jim?'

'The doctor says a week.'

'But they know where I am now and they'll come, they'll come! They want to kill me and take my sea-chest. Jim, did you see that Black Dog today? He's a bad man, but the others are very bad! And they want my sea-chest. You see, they are old Cap'n Flint's men and they want to know where his treasure is. They're going to give me the black spot!'

'What's the black spot?' I asked.

'They always give you the black spot before they kill you!'

That evening my poor father died. For a few days my mother I and were very busy and we didn't think much about the captain. The day after my father's funeral a blind man with a stick stopped outside the inn and asked me if it was called the "Admiral Benbow".

I said yes.

'Will you give me your hand, my young friend, and take me into the inn?'

When I gave him my hand he pulled me to him quickly.

'Now, boy! Take me to the captain!'

'I can't, sir,' I said.

'Oh? Take me or I'll break your arm!'

His voice was cold and cruel. I was very afraid of him and I took him to the captain. The poor old pirate was very afraid too.

'Now give me your left hand, Bill,' the blind man said.

And he put something in the captain's hand. Then he went out of the inn very fast. The captain looked at his left hand. There was a piece of paper with a black spot on it.

'Ten o'clock! They're coming at ten and they'll kill me. We've got six hours, Jim! We've still got time!'

The captain tried to stand up but just then he put his hand to his heart and fell on the floor. I ran to help him, but he was dead.

CHAPTER TWO

The Sea-chest

Now my mother and I decided to go to the village for help. When we arrived, the people didn't want to return with us to the inn. They were too afraid. My mother said angrily:

'Jim, we'll go back. We'll open the captain's sea-chest s and take our money.'

So a boy from the village went to find Dr Livesey and my mother and I went back to the "Admiral Benbow". I locked the door. The dead captain was still on the floor.

'We must find the key and open the chest,' said my mother.

I looked at the piece of paper near his hand. There was a message on it: 'We're coming tonight at ten.' I looked at the clock. It was six.

'We've got four hours, mother,' I said.

I found the key in the captain's pocket. We went upstairs to his room and my mother opened the chest. Inside there was a packet of papers and a bag. In the bag we found a lot of money and my mother started to count it. But then I heard the sound of the blind man's stick on the road. He tried to open the door but it was locked. Then he went away.

'We must go, mother,' I said. 'He'll tell the other men and they'll come here.'

'No,' she answered. 'It's only seven o'clock. The captain must pay the correct money for his stay with us.' And she continued to count the money.

But soon we heard the voices of the pirates. We took some money and the packet of papers, and we ran out of the inn. Suddenly my mother stopped.

'My dear, I can't run.'

'Oh mother!' I said angrily. 'Why did you count all that money? Now they're going to kill us.'

Then she fell on my shoulder. Fortunately, we were near a little bridge.

'Come, mother,' I said. 'There's a bridge. We'll go under it and the pirates won't see us.'

But I went back and stood behind a tree. I could see the road in front of our inn. Some men arrived. One of them was the blind man.

'Go in!' he shouted at the men.

They found the dead captain, and the sea-chest upstairs. One man opened the window of the captain's room.

'Pew! The chest is open!' he told the blind man.

'Is the packet of papers there?' said Pew.

'We can't see it.'

'The boy has got it!' said Pew. 'Look for them, you dogs! Find them and we'll all be rich!'

'But we can take some money and go, Pew,' said one man.

Now the blind man was very angry. He tried to hit the other pirates with his stick. Then I heard the sound of horses. The pirates ran away very fast. In a minute there was only Pew on the road.

'Don't leave me, mates!' he shouted.

Some men on horses came down the hill. Pew tried to run away but he couldn't see. He fell down, he got up, he ran... But he ran into one of the horses and he was killed.

The men on the horses were police officers. With them was the boy from the village.

'What did these pirates want?' one of the officers asked.

I replied. 'I think they wanted this.' And I showed him the packet of papers. 'I want to give it to Dr Livesey.'

'Yes, he's a good man. I'll take you to his house.'

Dr Livesey was at the Hall, Squire Trelawney's big house. The two men were in the library.

'Good evening, Jim,' said the doctor. 'What are you doing here?'

I told them everything. Then I gave the packet of papers to the doctor and he put it in his pocket. After the officer left, he said to the squire:

'Have you heard of a pirate called Captain Flint?'

'Yes. A terrible man! The Spanish were very afraid of him.'

'Did he have any money?'

'Don't you know the story of Flint's treasure? Nobody knows where he buried it.

'Very well,' said the doctor, and he opened the packet.

There were two things in it: a book and a piece of paper. On the first page of the book was the name 'Billy Bones, mate.'

Then there were a lot of dates and sums of money.

'This is an account book,' the doctor said. 'It shows how much money that buccaneer Billy Bones got.'

Then he opened the paper. It was a map of an island, about nine miles long and five miles wide. There were two big harbours, and a hill called "The Spy-glass". There were also three crosses: two on the north part of the island and one in the south-west. Next to this one were the words: 'A lot of the treasure here'.

'Livesey!' said Mr Trelawney happily. 'Tomorrow I'm going to Bristol to buy a ship and find some men. Hawkins, you'll be the cabin boy. You, Livesey, are the ship's doctor. We'll find the treasure, and we'll all be rich!'

The doctor answered, 'Jim and I will go with you. But the pirates also know about this paper and they want the treasure. So we mustn't say a word about this map.'

'Livesey, you're right,' said the squire. I won't say a word.'

CHAPTER THREE

Long John Silver

The squire went to Bristol and I lived at the Hall with Redruth, his servant. The weeks passed. Then a letter arrived from Squire Trelawney. It said that the ship was ready. Its name was Hispaniola and it was a very good ship. But there were problems. The squire could find only four men. Then he met a man called Long John Silver, a seaman, and gave him a job as cook on the ship. The letter continued:

'... He has only got one leg, but he's a fine man. He found some men for me. They're good, strong men. Now we've got a crew and I want to begin our voyage immediately! So come to Bristol quickly, Hawkins, with Redruth.'

The next morning Redruth and I travelled to Bristol. It was a wonderful city and a big port with lots of ships. I was very excited because I was going to sail to an island and find buried treasure!

When we saw the squire he said, 'The doctor is here. We're sailing tomorrow!'

Then he sent me to the "Spy-glass" inn with a note for John Silver. I knew Long John when I saw him because he had one leg. He was about fifty but very tall and strong. I remembered the old captain's words at the "Admiral Benbow": 'Tell me when you see a sailor with one leg.' Was that sailor Long John Silver?

'Mr Silver, sir?'

'Yes, my boy. And who are you?' Then he saw the note in my hand. 'Oh, you're our new cabin boy. Hello...'

At that moment a man ran out of the inn. I knew his face.

'Stop him!' I shouted. 'It's Black Dog! He's a pirate!'

'What!' Silver said. 'A pirate here in my inn! I don't know his name but I think I saw him here with a blind man.'

'Yes. I know that blind man. His name was Pew.'

I looked at Long John. Black Dog was here at his inn. I thought: 'Is Black Dog his friend? Was Pew his friend? Are the other buccaneers his friends?' But John Silver was a clever man. He smiled at me and he said:

'Look, Hawkins. This is bad for me. Black Dog was here and Squire Trelawney will think I'm a bad man. I'll come with you and talk to him.'

When Long John told the squire and Dr Livesey about Black Dog they believed him and thought that he was an honest man.

'We're sailing at four o'clock this afternoon, Silver,' the squire told him.

'Aye, aye, sir!' said the cook. And he went away.

When we went on board the Hispaniola the captain of the ship was angry. He wanted to speak to the squire.

'What is it, Captain Smollett?' said Mr Trelawney.

'I must tell you that I don't like this voyage; I don't like the men; and I don't like my officer.'

The squire was very angry, but Dr Livesey said:

'Why don't you like this voyage, captain?'

'The squire didn't tell me that we are going to look for treasure. I heard about it from the men. I don't like treasure voyages. They are dangerous - very dangerous.'

'I understand,' the doctor said. 'But why don't you like the crew? Aren't they all good seamen?'

'Perhaps,' replied the captain. 'But I don't like them.'

'All right. In your opinion, captain, what must we do?' 'First, you must put the guns, the powder and the ammunition near this cabin. Second, there are four good men - your men, Squire. They can sleep here, near your cabin.'

When Captain Smollett went out, the doctor said, 'Trelawney, you have two honest men on this ship - Captain Smollett and John Silver.'

'John Silver - yes!' said the squire angrily. 'But not the captain, not him!'

When Long John Silver came on board he said. 'What's happening, mates?'

'We're putting the guns and ammunition near the squire's cabin,' answered one of the men.

'Why?'

Just then the captain arrived. 'My orders!' he said. 'Now go down and cook the supper, my man!'

'Aye, aye, sir!' answered Long John, and he went to the kitchen.

'He's a good man,' the doctor said to the captain.

'Perhaps, sir.' Then the captain saw me and said, 'Go down to the kitchen and help the cook!'

I really didn't like Captain Smollett.

Early in the morning the ship was ready and we began our voyage to the Island of Treasure.

John Silver could move very fast around the ship on his one leg. His friend Israel Hands told me, 'He's very courageous - like a lion!' All the men liked him. He did his work well. To me he was always kind and he was always happy when I came to the kitchen. In one corner he had a parrot in a cage.

'Welcome, Jim!' he said one day. 'My parrot Cap'n Flint says our voyage will be good.'

'Pieces of eight! Pieces of eight!' said the parrot.

'You know, that bird is maybe two hundred years old,' Long John said, and he gave it some sugar. 'She has sailed to many places - Madagascar,

Malabar...'

And he told me wonderful stories about Captain Flint. I liked John Silver very much, and I thought he was a very good man.

Captain Smollett was happy with the Hispaniola. And now he also said that the men were good. But he didn't like no the voyage for treasure; and he didn't like the squire. So the squire didn't like him.

One evening, just before we arrived at Treasure Island, I wanted to eat an apple before I went to bed. The apples were in some big barrels on deck. In one barrel there weren't many apples, so I climbed into it. I ate an apple but I was very tired and I fell asleep. I woke up when I heard John Silver's voice. He was very near the barrel. I heard only a few words and then I began to tremble. 'Flint was my captain,' said Long John to a young man called Dick. 'We were all pirates - me and Pew and the others. I lost my leg and Pew lost his eyes. But I put a lot of money in the bank. Look at Pew: he was rich and then he became poor. And where is he now? Dead. And where are Flint's men now? Well, a lot of them are on this ship.'

I trembled when I heard this.

'I'm fifty years old,' Silver continued. 'After this voyage I'm going to live like a gentleman. You can be rich too, Dick, if you help old Long John. What do you say, my boy? Give me your hand.'

Now I understood. This young man was honest, but now he was one of Silver's men. Then I heard the voice of Israel Hands, Silver's friend.

'Look, I want to know something. How long must we wait? I want to kill that Captain Smollett. But when, Silver - when?'

'You're not very clever, Israel,' answered Silver. 'You must wait. I'll tell you when. The squire and the doctor have got the map. They'll find the treasure and put it on the ship - for us! So we'll wait.'

'But,' said Dick, 'What will we do with the captain, the squire and the doctor?'

'That's a good question!' the cook answered. 'Well, what do you think? We can leave them on the island, or we can kill them. Flint and Billy Bones always killed people. So I say to you, mates - wait, and then... kill them! Dick, get me an apple from this barrel.'

I felt very afraid when I heard this. But I couldn't move. Dick came near the barrel. Then Israel Hands said:

'Don't eat those bad apples! Let's drink some rum!'

When Dick returned with the rum the pirates drank.

Then a voice shouted, 'Land-ho!'

CHAPTER FOUR

The Island

The pirates ran to look at the land. Quickly I climbed out of the barrel and followed them. In the light of the moon we could see two hills.

'Who knows this land?' Captain Smollett asked the crew.

'Me, sir!' said Long John.

The captain showed him a map of the island. 'Is this the place?'

Long John looked at the map with big eyes. But it wasn't the map from Billy Bones's chest; it was a copy, and there weren't any red crosses on it. Silver was angry but he didn't show it. He smiled.

'Yes, sir, this is the place.'

I wanted to tell my story to the captain, the squire and the doctor. When Dr Livesey asked me to go to the cabin and bring his pipe and tobacco, I said:

'Doctor, I must speak to you. I have terrible news.'

The doctor's face changed, but he said, 'Thank you, Jim.

Go down to the cabin now.'

And then he went to the squire and the captain and spoke to them quietly.

'Men!' the captain said to the crew. 'The doctor and I are going down to the cabin to drink some wine!'

Down in the cabin I told them everything about Silver's conversation. They looked at me; they didn't move or speak. When I stopped, Mr Trelawney said to the captain: 'You were right and I was wrong. What can we do?' 'We've got time because Silver is clever and he'll wait,' said the captain. 'I think we must attack the pirates first. How many men have we got?'

'Seven, including Jim,' said the doctor. 'How many honest men are there in the crew?'

'There are the four men that the squire found before he met Silver,' the captain said.

'But,' said Mr Trelawney, 'Israel Hands was one of them.'

'Well, we don't know how many men are good.'

'Jim can help us,' said Dr Livesey. 'The men like him and talk to him. He can tell us who is honest or bad.'

There were only seven men out of twenty-six. And I was only a boy, so there were six adult men against nineteen pirates.

Next morning I looked at the island. I saw tall trees and yellow sand. The hills were high, but Spyglass hill was very high. Our ship went towards a small island called Skeleton Island. The men prepared the boats.

It was hot and they didn't like the work. They spoke angrily. We knew they wanted to kill us. But Long John smiled and spoke to them and sang. He helped to take the ship into the big harbour between Skeleton Island and Treasure Island.

The captain, the doctor, Mr Trelawney and I went to the cabin. We gave pistols to the three honest men: Hunter, Joyce and Redruth. Then the captain went on deck and told the crew that they could go on the island for the afternoon.

'Hurray!' shouted the men. They were happy now.

They thought that the treasure was already in their hands.

Six men stayed on the ship. Thirteen, including Silver, got into the boats. Then I had a crazy idea. I decided to go to the island in one of the boats. I didn't say anything to the doctor and the squire. When I climbed into the boat, nobody saw me.

My boat arrived first. I got out and ran fast into the trees. A long way behind me Long John Silver shouted,

'Jim, Jim!' But I ran and ran.

I stopped and looked around me. There were strange trees and flowers, and birds. The sun was hot. I could see Spy-glass hill in front of me.

Then I heard voices and I went behind a tree. One of the voices was John Silver's. Now I was very afraid. I thought: 'Jim, you were stupid to come to the island with these pirates. But you must help the doctor and the others.' So I moved towards the pirates on my hands and knees.

'Tom,' said Silver, 'I like you, mate, and I want to help you!'

The other man answered, 'Silver, you're honest. I'm sure you don't want to be with these bad pirates - not you!'

So this Tom was one of the honest men!

Suddenly there was a long, terrible scream. It came from far away.

'What was that, John?' said Tom.

Long John smiled. 'That? That was Alan. He's dead now.'

'They've killed Alan!' Tom said. 'John Silver, you were my friend, but not now. Kill me too - if you can!'

Then brave Tom walked away with his back to the cook. But he didn't go far. Silver held the branch of a tree and he threw his crutch. It hit Tom's back like a missile. He fell, and in a moment Silver killed him with his knife.

I couldn't believe it. Now two honest men were dead! Then Silver called the other pirates. I ran away very fast. I thought: 'They'll kill me. Good-bye to the Hispaniola; good-bye to the squire, the doctor and the captain!'

I was very near Spy-glass hill. There were a lot of trees around me, like a forest. Suddenly I heard a noise behind a tree. What was it? I didn't know and I stopped in terror.

Behind me were the pirates; in front of me was this - thing! I preferred the pirates and I began to run back. But the thing began to run too! It ran from tree to tree - on two legs! It was a man. Was he a cannibal? I took my pistol and I walked towards him. Slowly he moved from behind a tree and he came towards me. Then suddenly he fell on his knees and he put his hands towards me. I asked him who he was.

'Ben Gunn.' he answered in a strange voice.

I saw that he was a white man. His eyes were blue, but his face was very dark from the sun. His clothes were old and dirty.

He said, 'You're the first Christian I've seen for three years!'

'What happened?' I asked.

'I was marooned'

I knew this was a horrible thing. The buccaneers left him on the island - to live or to die.

'What's your name, mate?' he asked.

I told him.

'Well, Jim, many years ago I was a good boy like you.

But then I became bad and I drank a lot of rum. And here I am on this desert island,' Then he looked around him and said in a quiet voice, 'Jim, I'm rich!'

I thought, 'He's crazy, poor man!'

'Rich, rich, I tell you! But wait, Jim. Is that Flint's ship down there?'

'No. Flint is dead. But some of the crew are Flint's men.'

'A man with one leg?' Ben Gunn asked, very frightened.

'Yes, John Silver. He's the cook and the chief of the pirates.'

Then I told him about our voyage and our difficult situation.

He said, 'Well, Ben Gunn will help you. And then... do you think your squire will help me perhaps?'

'Yes, he's a gentleman.'

'And will he take me to England on the ship?'

'Oh yes, I'm sure!'

'Good!' Ben Gunn said happily. 'I'll tell you something.

I was on Flint's ship when he buried the treasure - with six big, strong seamen. Then he killed the six seamen. Well, Billy Bones and Long John asked him where the treasure was, but he didn't tell them. Then, three years ago I was on another ship near this island. "Boys, let's go and find Flint's treasure!" I said. But we couldn't find it. So the other men were angry with me and they left me on the island. You must tell the squire all this. Tell him I'm not a pirate - eh, Jim? Tell him I'm a good man.'

'But how can I?' I said. 'I can't go on the ship now.' 'True,' he said. 'But I've got a boat, Jim. I made it with my two hands. It's under the white rock.'

At that moment there was a great sound of cannons. 'The battle has begun!' I said. 'Quick, follow me!'

And I began to run towards the harbour where the Hispaniola was. Ben Gunn came with me. We could hear the sounds of a battle. Then I saw the British flag - the Union Jack - in the air above the trees.

CHAPTER FIVE

The Doctor Continues the Story

After the two boats left the Hispaniola, the captain, the squire and I talked in the cabin. Then Hunter came and told us that Jim Hawkins was on the island with the pirates.

'Poor Jim,' said the squire. 'They'll find him and kill him.'

We ran on deck and saw the two boats near a river with two men in them. We decided to go to the island. But first we looked at the map. There was a stockade on it.

'Hunter,' I said, 'you and I will go and find this stockade.'

We got into a boat. The two pirates near the river saw us, but they didn't do anything. We went towards the beach where the stockade was. When we arrived,

I got out of the boat and ran fast into the trees. The stockade was there, on top of a small hill. Inside, there was a large wooden cabin with holes in the walls for guns. Around the cabin was a high wall made of wood. With food and water we could stay in this stockade, safe from the pirates.

Then I heard a terrible sound: it was the cry of a person at the moment of death.

'Jim Hawkins! Poor boy!' I thought. 'They've killed him!' And I was very sad.

When we arrived back at the ship the others also thought Jim was dead. Then we put lots of things in the boat: guns, powder, ammunition, meat, biscuits and cognac. There were six pirates on board. One of them was Israel Hands. With two pistols in his hands the captain called him.

'Don't do anything stupid, Hands - or we'll kill you!'

The six men ran away and hid in another part of the ship.

When our boat was ready, we all got in and went towards the island. The men in the boats saw us and one of them ran to tell Long John Silver. At the stockade we put the things in the cabin. Then the captain, Redruth and I went back to the Hispaniola and took more provisions.

We worked very fast. Then the captain called to one of the pirates on the ship.

'Gray!' he said. 'You're a good man - I know. Come with us. You've got thirty seconds.'

There was silence. Then we heard sounds of a fight, and suddenly Abraham Gray ran towards us.

'I'm with you, sir!' he said.

Our boat was small. There were five men and a lot of things in it. The current was different now; it took us away from our beach.

'We will never arrive at the stockade,' I said.

'Look! Behind us - on the ship!' said the captain.

The five men on the ship were busy with a big cannon. They were going to fire at us.

'Mr Trelawney,' said the captain. 'Shoot Israel Hands.'

The squire fired his gun. But he didn't kill Hands; one of the other men fell. Now we saw a lot of pirates in one of the boats near the river.

'The pirates are coming!' said the captain.

'Only one of the boats is coming,' I said. 'Perhaps the other pirates are running to the stockade.'

'Perhaps,' the captain said. 'But I'm frightened of that cannon! They're going to fire it.'

We were very near the beach when the pirates fired. The cannon ball passed over our heads. Then our boat went under the water. At that moment we heard some pirates in the woods. They were very near the stockade, where there were only two men: Hunter and Joyce.

'Hurry, hurry!' said the captain.

And we ran quickly up the little hill towards the stockade. But the buccaneers were just behind us. Seven of them ran fast towards us. The squire and I fired our pistols and killed one of them. But Tom Redruth was shot. We took him into the stockade and put him on the floor of the cabin. And there brave Redruth died. We were all very sad. Suddenly a cannon ball exploded inside the stockade. All that evening ball after ball fell, but they didn't hit us. Israel Hands couldn't see the stockade, but he could see the Union Jack above the cabin. That was dangerous.

'We must take it down, captain,' said the squire.

But the captain said no.

Two men went to the beach to bring the things from our boat. But the pirates were already there and they were taking our things.

The captain wrote in his log-book:

'There are six of us now: Captain Smollett; Dr Livesey; Abraham Gray; Squire Trelawney; John Hunter and Richard Joyce. We came to this stockade on Treasure Island and we have got provisions for ten days. Thomas Redruth, the squire's servant, was shot by the buccaneers. Jim Hawkins, cabin boy.

CHAPTER SIX

Jim Hawkins Continues the Story

When Ben Gunn saw the Union Jack, he stopped. 'That's Flint's old stockade,' he said. 'Are your friends there?'

'I don't know,' I replied. 'Perhaps it's the pirates.'

'No. Their flag is the Jolly Roger. It's your friends.' 'Good! Now I can go to them,' I said. 'Are you coining with me?'

'No, mate. Old Ben Gunn isn't stupid! First, you must tell the squire about me, and he must promise to help me. Tell him to come and find me.'

'All right. I'm going now.' in different directions.

For an hour a lot of cannon balls fell. I was very frightened and stayed in the woods. In the evening I arrived at the beach and I saw the Hispaniola with the black Jolly Roger - the pirates' flag!

The bombardment stopped. I waited for a while, and then I decided to go to the stockade. When I stood up, I saw a high, white rock in some trees near the sea. 'That's Ben Gunn's white rock,' I thought. 'Now I know where his boat is.' Then I ran to the stockade.

I told my story to my friends in the cabin. When I finished, it was evening and the wind was cold. I was very tired, but the captain gave us all some work. Two men went to find wood for the fire and the doctor cooked some food. I was a guard at the door. After a while, the doctor talked to me about Ben Gunn. He wanted to know where he was.

He said, 'I've got a piece of Italian Parmesan cheese. It's very good. I'd like to give it to Ben Gunn.'

After our dinner, we talked.

There was only a little food, so we knew that we must kill the pirates quickly. We could hear them. They were sitting by the river about half a mile away. They were singing round a fire. I was very tired and I fell asleep. When I woke up there were voices.

'Look! It's Long John Silver!' somebody said. 'He's coming here with a white flag. He wants to talk.'

The captain said, 'Stay here, men! Guns ready!' Then he called to the pirate. 'What do you want?'

'Cap'n Silver wants to speak to you,' said John Silver. 'Captain Silver? I don't know him. Who's he?'

'The men said I'm cap'n now - after you left the ship, sir. Can we talk?'

'I don't want to talk with you, Silver. You can come in if you want, but don't try to do anything stupid.'

'I give you my word, sir.'

So Silver threw his crutch over the wall. He only had one leg but he climbed into the stockade very well. Then he came up the small hill and arrived at the cabin. The captain told him to sit down.

'On the sand?' Silver said.

'Yes, on the sand, Silver. You can't come into the cabin. Now, what do you want to say?'

Long John sat down. 'You did very well last night, cap'n. My men and I were very surprised. You came and killed one of them. He was full of rum and he was asleep. But you won't do it again, cap'n!'

The captain didn't understand this. But I remembered Ben Gunn. Did he kill one of the pirates last night? Well, now there were only thirteen of them. Silver continued: 'You've got the map. We want it, cap'n.'

The captain smoked his pipe calmly. 'We know that, my man. But you can't have it.'

Long John was angry. But he smoked his pipe too.

'Now, here's my idea, cap'n,' he said. 'You give us the map. When we get the treasure on the ship you can sail with us. I give you my word that you'll be safe. But if you don't like that idea, you can stay here and we'll give you some of our food. When I see a ship. I'll tell the captain to come here. What do you say, Cap'n Smollett?'

'Is that all?' the captain said. 'Now you listen to me, Silver. You must come here with all your pirates - and without any guns. I promise I'll take you to England for a fair trial. If you don't do this, we'll kill you - all of you! Now go - quickly!'

Silver was furious. He stood up with his crutch.

'You dogs! You're laughing now, but I'm coming back with my men! We'll kill you all!'

Alter he went out of the stockade, the captain spoke to us.

'In an hour Silver will come back with his men,' he said. 'There are thirteen of them; we are six - and Jim. But we can beat them! Hawkins, eat your breakfast. Hunter, brandy for everyone. Trelawney, put out the fire. Doctor, you will be at the door. Hunter, you will be on the east side of the cabin. Joyce, west. Trelawney, you and Gray go to the north side. Hawkins, you and I will load the guns.'

An hour passed. We waited nervously. Then Joyce suddenly saw the pirates and fired his gun. The pirates fired at us; then they stopped. All was quiet again.

'How many shots did you see, doctor?' asked the captain.

'Three.'

'Mr Trelawney?'

'About seven.'

'So they're attacking from the north.'

The captain was right. A few minutes later, a lot of pirates came out of the woods to the north. They ran towards the stockade and climbed over the wall. The squire and Gray fired their guns. They killed two pirates. But four of them ran toward us. One pirate attacked the doctor.

The captain shouted, 'Fight them outside the cabin with cutlasses!'

Quickly I took a cutlass and ran out of the cabin. Gray was behind me. The doctor killed his attacker. I ran to the left and I saw a pirate. Suddenly I fell. The pirate was going to kill me. But Gray ran from behind me and killed him. Now four pirates were dead. The other one ran away and escaped. The doctor, Gray and I ran back quickly to the cabin.

Hunter was dead, and Joyce died later. The captain was wounded.

'How many of them are dead?' he asked the doctor.

'Five, including the pirate last night.'

'That's good! Now there are four of us against eight of them.'

CHAPTER SEVEN

My Sea Adventure

The pirates didn't return. While the squire and I cooked dinner, the doctor helped the captain.

'Your wound isn't dangerous,' he told him. 'But you must rest.'

After dinner the doctor put on his hat and took his pistols. He also took a cutlass and a map. And he left the stockade and went into the woods.

'What's he doing?' Gray asked me.

'I think he's going to find Ben Gunn.'

'He's crazy!' laughed Gray.

Then I also did something crazy! It was very hot in the stockade now. There was a lot of blood; there were dead men. I began to feel bad. I wanted to leave and go into the woods, like the doctor. So I put a lot of biscuits in my pockets and I took two pistols. Then I ran out of the stockade and into the trees. Nobody saw me.

Yes, I was crazy! But I was only a boy - and you will see that I helped to save all of us! I decided to find Ben Gunn's boat, so I went towards the white rock. I could see the Hispaniola in the harbour to my right. I ran quickly to the white rock and I looked for Ben Gunn's boat. I found it - a very small, light boat. There was also a paddle.

Now I had another crazy idea! I decided to go to the Hispaniola, and cut her anchor rope. Then she would go towards the beach and stop there, so the pirates couldn't escape. It was very dark now, but I could just see the pirates' big fire near the river and the lights of the Hispaniola I took the little boat down to the sea.

The current was strong and it carried me fast towards the Hispaniola. When I was near her, I took the anchor rope in my hand. It was very rigid. I thought: 'This rope is dangerous. I mustn't cut it or it will hit me.'

But I was lucky because the wind changed and the ship moved towards me. Now the rope wasn't rigid and I could cut it. At that moment I heard voices in the captain's cabin. It was Israel Hands and a pirate with a red cap. They were drunk. They were also angry, and each man was shouting at the other. When I cut the rope, the Hispaniola began to move round with the current. I paddled towards the window of Captain Smollett's cabin to watch Hands and his companion. I climbed up a rope and I saw a terrible fight between the two men. They wanted to kill each other.

I went down the rope to the boat. Suddenly the current changed again. The ship and my little boat turned and went towards the island. The pirates' camp fire was very near! Then the ship turned again and went away from me very fast. I was now alone in my little boat. The waves were strong and high. I was very wet and cold. I sat there in terror. Tin going to die soon,' I thought. But sleep soon came to me and I dreamed of home.

It was day when I woke up. My boat was at the southwest end of the island. I wasn't far from land but there were cliffs and big rocks. Then I remembered the map. I knew there was a good place called Cape of the Woods to the north. I also remembered that the map showed a strong north current. So I decided to stop at the Cape of the Woods.

My little boat went up and down on the big waves and I was very frightened. I paddled slowly. It was hard work and I became tired and thirsty. Then I saw the trees of the Cape of the Woods. But the current was very strong and it took me past the Cape. Suddenly I saw the Hispaniola in front of me about half a mile away. 'Now the pirates will kill me!' I thought. But the ship was moving strangely. She sailed and stopped, sailed and stopped; and she turned north, south, east, west. I watched her with surprise. And then I understood! The two pirates were drunk or asleep. I had an idea: 'Perhaps I can go on board and take her to the captain.' So I paddled towards her, and when I came near to her, I jumped on to the bowsprit above me. My boat went under the water. But now I was on the Hispaniola!

Was there anybody on board? I heard only the sound of the ship when she turned in the wind. Then I saw the two pirates on deck. Perhaps they were asleep. But when I saw some blood on the deck, I was sure they were dead. Then Israel Hands moved.

'Brandy!' he said in a weak voice.

I went down to the captain's cabin. There were lots of empty bottles. I found one with some brandy, and I took some biscuits and cheese and went up on deck. I drank a lot of water from the water barrel and then I gave the brandy to Hands. He drank a lot quickly.

I sat down and began to eat. 'What happened here?' I asked.

Hands looked at the man with the red cap. 'Well, that dirty dog is dead,' he replied. 'What are you doing here?'

'This ship is mine now, Mr Hands, so please call me captain.'

He looked at me but he didn't speak. When I took down the black pirate flag, he said, 'Shall we talk, Captain Hawkins? Me and this man here - O'Brien - we wanted to sail the ship back to the harbour, where she was before.

But - well, he's dead now. Who is going to sail her? You? No, you can't do it. Give me food and drink, and something for my wound. Then I'll tell you how to sail her.'

'We're not going back to the harbour,' I answered. Tin sailing the ship to North Inlet and I'm going to take her on to the beach there.'

'North Inlet? Yes, I'll help you to sail her there.'

'All right, tell me what I must do.'

And in a few minutes the Hispaniola began to sail north.

I put a handkerchief on Hand's leg. He ate and he drank more brandy. Soon he was better. The ship was dirty and I cleaned it. But the eyes of the pirate watched me, and he smiled sometimes - a strange, bad smile.

We sailed fast along the north of the island towards North Inlet. But we couldn't take the ship on the beach immediately, so we waited for the tide to change. Then Hands spoke.

'Cap'n,' he said with a strange smile. 'Will you go to the cabin and bring me a bottle of wine? This brandy is too strong.'

I didn't believe this and I knew that he had a plan; but I also knew that he was stupid.

So I went down below, but I didn't go to the cabin. I went to a place where I could watch Hands. And I was right! He went across the deck on his hands and knees. In front of him there was a circle of rope. He took a long knife out of it. The knife had blood on it.

He put it in his pocket. So Israel Hands wanted to kill me! But I was safe for the moment. 'He won't kill me now.' I thought. 'He'll wait, because he can't bring the ship on to the beach without me.'

I took the wine to Hands and he drank some of it.

'Jim, cut me some tobacco,' he said. 'I haven't got a knife. Ah, Jim, I'm going to die. Cut me my last piece of tobacco.'

So I cut him a piece. 'You're a bad man, Mr Hands,' I said.

'Oh? Why, Jim?'

'Why? You killed this man O'Brien!'

He answered, 'Because I know that dead men don't kill - amen! Now, Cap'n Hawkins, you listen to my orders and we'll sail this ship on to the beach.'

It was difficult, but Hands was a very good pilot. We went into North Inlet where the water was calm.

'There!' said Hands. 'I can see a good beach. We'll put the ship there.'

At the right moment he said: 'Now! Beach her now, Jim!'

When the Hispaniola began to go fast towards the beach, I was excited - and I forgot about Israel Hands! He was behind me. Perhaps I heard something and I suddenly turned my head. Hands was there, with his knife in his right hand. He was going to kill me and I shouted in terror. When he came towards me, I ran behind the mast and took a pistol from my pocket. I tried to fire it at Hands but it was wet with sea water. He came towards me. His face was red with anger.

Just then the Hispaniola hit the beach. She fell on her side at an angle of 45 degree and Hands and I fell with her. I was on my feet very quickly. But now I couldn't run away because the deck was at a 45 degree angle. Quickly I jumped on to the mast and climbed to the top. I sat on the cross tree and waited for Hands.

He looked up at me and he didn't know what to do. I loaded my two pistols. Then, with the knife in his mouth, Hands began to climb the mast.

'Don't come up, Mr Hands, or I'll kill you!' I said.

He stopped. He tried to think, but he was slow and stupid. Then he took the knife from his mouth and said:

'Jim, I must kill you, but it's difficult for me to kill a boy like you.'

And suddenly his right hand moved fast and the next moment the knife went into my shoulder. My two pistols fired; then they fell from my hands. There was a cry and I looked down. Israel Hands was falling into the water. Then he was on the sand on the bottom of the sea. And he was dead.

The knife was in my shoulder. There was a lot of blood on my coat and shirt. I felt very bad. When I tried to take the knife out, I began to tremble - and then suddenly it came out. I climbed down the mast and went to the cabin. My wound was small and it wasn't dangerous. I cleaned it and put a handkerchief round it. Then I went up to the deck. It was evening now and I decided to go to the island.

I wanted to tell Captain Smollett and the others about my adventure. I wanted to tell them that the ship was ours now. So I left the ship and began to walk in the direction of the stockade.

The night was very dark and it was difficult for me to see. Then the moon came up and I found the stockade. When I saw the red light of a fire outside the cabin, I stopped. This was strange; my companions usually made a fire inside the cabin. Slowly, quietly, I went towards the cabin on my hands and knees. At the door I stood up and looked inside. It was dark. I couldn't see anything. I walked in - and suddenly a strange voice said: 'Pieces of eight! Pieces of eight! Pieces of eight!'

Captain Flint, Silver's parrot! I wanted to run away but there was no time.

'Who's there?' shouted Silver.

I turned, I ran away. But I ran into the arms of one of the pirates.

CHAPTER EIGHT

In Silver's Comp

'Bring a torch, Dick!' Silver said.

Dick went out and brought a piece of wood from the fire. Now I saw my terrible situation: Silver and his men had the stockade; my companions weren't there. And I was a prisoner.

'Well!' said Long John. 'Jim Hawkins has come to visit us. That's a nice surprise for old John.' And he began to smoke his pipe. 'I've always liked you, Jim boy.' Silver continued. 'You've got courage. But now you're going to die. Your friends won't help you. You ran away and you can't go back to them. They don't want you.'

So my friends were alive! I was very happy about this.

'So you can decide, Jim,' Silver said. 'What do you want: to be with us - or to die?'

Death was very near now, and I was frightened. 'Before I decide, can you tell me what happened here, and where my friends are?' I asked.

Silver replied, 'Yesterday morning Dr Livesey came to us with a white flag. He said to me, "The ship has gone. You're finished, Cap'n Silver." I looked and - yes, it was true. The ship wasn't there! "All right, doctor," I said. "We'll talk." So we talked. And here we are in the cabin with lots of food and brandy and wood for the fire. Your friends went away. I don't know where they are. And you, Jim? Well, I said to the doctor, "How many are you?" "Four," he replied. "One is wounded. And we don't want to see Jim Hawkins again. He ran away and he can die if he wants!" Those were his words, Jim.'

'Well, I know you're going to kill me,' I began, 'But first I want to tell you my story. Here you are - no ship, no treasure, and a lot of men dead. Do you want to know who did it? It was I! I was in the apple barrel when you talked that night with Hands, and Dick, and the others. And it was I that cut the Hispaniola's anchor. It was I that killed Israel Hands. It was I that took the ship to a place where you'll never find her. I'm not frightened of you, John Silver. Kill me if you want. But if you kill me, you won't have a witness I when you're captured. If I live, I'll help you and

I'll save your lives.'

Then one of the pirates called Morgan took his knife.

'Now you must die!' he said to me.

'Stop there!' shouted Silver. 'Who are you, Tom Morgan? Are you the cap'n here? No! I'm the cap'n - and don't forget it!'

'Tom is right,' said another pirate. 'You can go to hell, Silver!'

'Do you want to fight with me?' Silver shouted in a terrible voice. 'Take a cutlass, all of you - if you want to die! Well, I'm waiting! Who wants to die?'

Not one man moved; not one man answered.

'Well, I'm cap'n here because I can fight better than all of you,' continued Silver. 'I like that boy. He's got a lot of courage - more courage than all of you! So? Who is going to kill him - eh?'

There was a long silence. Silver stood near me. He smoked his pipe and watched the others.

Then one of them said, 'We want to go outside and talk about this.'

And the pirates walked out of the cabin.

'Listen, Jim,' Silver said quietly. 'They're going to kill me. Then they'll kill you. But I want to help you. A moment ago, when you spoke with a lot of courage, I decided to help you. You help Hawkins and he'll help you, I thought. The ship has gone and we're all finished. But I'll save your life and you'll save mine.'

'I'll do what I can,' I said.

'Good boy, Jim! Listen. I'm not stupid. I'm with the squire now. You've got the ship. I don't know how you did it, but I know when I've lost. I'm with you now.' Silver took some cognac from a barrel. 'Drink with me, Jim! They're going to come back soon and then...' He looked at the door nervously. Then he said, 'Why did the doctor give me the map, Jim?'

I didn't understand and I looked surprised.

'Yes, he gave me the map,' Long John said. 'Why?'

Just then we heard the buccaneers outside. The door opened and the five men came in. One of them walked slowly towards us. He had something in his right hand.

'Come on, I won't eat you!' said Long John.

The buccaneer gave a piece of paper to Silver. He looked at it.

'The black spot!' he said.

'Yes, John Silver!' said a buccaneer called George.

'You've got the black spot. You're finished now. You're not a good cap'n. You did things badly. You talked with the doctor and now they're free. And then there's this boy. We're going to be arrested, we'll all die on the gallows. And why? Because you did things badly!'

'Me? Well, you didn't do what I wanted, you didn't listen to me. And now look at our situation! We'll all die on the gallows in London. Who did it? You did it! And now you want to kill me?'

Silver was very angry and his voice was strong. The pirates listened well.

'We're all going to die and the birds will eat us,' he continued. 'Thanks to you! And the boy? He's our prisoner, he's our hostage. Are we going to kill our hostage? He'll help us when we're prisoners in London. He's our last hope! Kill him? Not I, mates! Look at you, John. You're wounded. And you,

George, you're ill with fever. So what did I do? I didn't kill the doctor. No, I talked with him, and now he comes every day and helps you. Did I do things badly? Well, look - look at this!'

And Long John threw a map on the floor. It was Billy Bones's map, with the three red crosses. When I saw it, I thought, 'Why did the doctor give it to Silver?'

The pirates ran quickly towards it. They took it and they laughed and shouted. But George said:

'How can we take the treasure with us? We haven't got the ship.'

'And who lost the ship?' Silver shouted at him. 'I got the map and you lost the ship! But I did things badly - eh? Speak to me politely, George Merry, or I'll kill you!'

'He's right,' said Morgan.

'Of course I'm right. But I don't want to be your cap'n. Find another cap'n.'

'No!' the pirates shouted. 'We want you, John!'

'Well, mates, what shall I do with this black spot? I don't want it. Jim, you have it - a present from old John.' That was the end of the conversation. After we all drank some brandy, we were ready to sleep. But I didn't sleep immediately. I thought about Silver and his difficult game. He didn't want to die on the gallows; he wanted to save his own life. He was a bad man but I was sorry for him. His situation was very dangerous.

I woke up when I heard the guard's voice outside early next morning. Dr Livesey was coming! I was happy; but I couldn't look at his face. I remembered that he didn't want to see me again.

'Good morning, doctor, sir!' said Long John with a big smile. 'Jim Hawkins is here.'

'Not Jim!' said the doctor, and he stopped, surprised. Then he came into the cabin. He looked at me quickly; and he didn't smile. He helped the man with the wound.

'Did you take your medicine?' he asked George Merry.

'Ay, ay, sir,' said Merry.

'Good. I'm a pirates' doctor now and I don't want to lose any of you for the trial in London. Well, I've finished for today. And now I want to talk with that boy, please.'

'No!' shouted George Merry, red with anger.

'Silence!' Silver shouted. 'Doctor, thank you for your help. Hawkins, will you give me your word that you will not run away?'

I gave Silver my word.

'Doctor, go outside the stockade. Jim will stay inside and stand near the wall. Then you can talk to him.'

When the doctor left the cabin the men were very angry with Silver. They told him that they understood his game very well.

'We made peace with the doctor and his friends,' he said. 'But when we're ready we can break it. Then I'll kill that doctor - believe me!'

So we went to the wall of the stockade. The other pirates watched us angrily.

At the wall Silver said, 'Do you see this, doctor?' I'm helping Jim. He'll tell you that I saved his life. This game is very dangerous for me. Remember that, and help me when you can.'

Silver's voice trembled. I saw that his face was white.

'Are you frightened, John?' the doctor asked.

'Doctor, I'm not frightened of anything. But I don't want to die on the gallows in London. You're an honest man.

You won't forget that Long John helped you.'

Then he went away and sat down on the sand.

The doctor began sadly, 'Hello, Jim. You're with these pirates now and you can see what happens when you do stupid things. You ran away when the captain was ill and wounded. That was bad!'

Then I began to cry. 'I'm very sorry! I know that I did a stupid thing, and now I'm a prisoner. Oh doctor! I'm really frightened...!'

Now the doctor wasn't angry. 'Jim! Climb over the wall quickly and we'll run!'

'But I gave Silver my word.'

'It doesn't matter now. You mustn't stay here. Come on, jump!'

'No, you know I can't, doctor. But listen. I took the ship to North Inlet. She's on the southern beach.'

I told the doctor quickly about my adventure. When I finished, he said:

'Oh Jim! You always save our lives! And now we must save yours. Listen, Ben Gunn told us something...' But then the doctor stopped and called Silver. He said to him, 'You must look for the treasure slowly. And you must be very careful when you find it. There will be problems.'

'Sir, I don't understand you. What is your game? Why did you leave the cabin? Why did you give me the map? And now you say look for the treasure slowly. Why? You say there'll be problems when we find it. What do you mean?'

T can't tell you now, Silver. I'm sorry. But I can tell you that I'll help you a lot when we return to London. I'll save your life if I can.'

John Silver looked very happy. 'Thank you, sir!'

'But you must help Jim now. He's your responsibility, Silver. Do you understand? Now I must go. Good-bye, Jim.'

And Dr Livesey went away.

CHAPTER NINE

The Treasure Hunt

'Jim,' said Silver. 'I heard the doctor when he said, "Jump over the wall and run." You didn't do it. You saved my life and I won't forget it. But now we must look for the treasure. I don't like treasure hunts. They're dangerous. You must stay very close to me.'

When we ate a breakfast of bacon and biscuits with the other pirates, Silver said to them:

'Mates, you're lucky because you've got old John and he thinks a lot. The others have got the ship and we don't know where it is. When we get the treasure, we'll find the ship. We've got the boats and we've got our hostage here.

But when we get the ship and the treasure, we'll kill him and the others.'

I was frightened and I couldn't eat my breakfast. Why did my friends leave the stockade? I thought. Why did they give Silver the map? Why did the doctor say, 'There will be problems when you find the treasure'? I couldn't find any answers to these questions.

So the treasure hunt began. Silver had two guns, a big cutlass and two pistols in the pockets of his coat. His parrot sat on his shoulder and talked. And I walked behind him with a rope round my neck.

First we went to the beach and got into the two boats. Silver looked at the map. On the back were these words:

Tall tree, Spy-glass hill.

Points to the north-east.

Skeleton Island south-east.

'First we must find a tall tree,' said Silver.

We went along the coast and after a while we saw a high plateau near Spy-glass hill with a lot of trees on it. Some of the trees were very tall, so when we saw a good place to stop, we got out of the boats and began to climb towards the plateau. We went up slowly. Suddenly one of the men in front of us shouted. We ran towards him.

'Has he found the treasure?' said Morgan.

'No,' said another man. 'He's very frightened.'

Then we saw a human skeleton under a big tree and we all became cold with terror.

'He was a seaman,' said George Merry.

'Look at the arms and hands and feet,' said Silver. 'They aren't in a natural position.'

He was right. The skeleton's feet pointed in one direction. The arms and the hands pointed in the opposite direction.

'I think I understand,' said Silver. 'Look, it's pointing south-east - at Skeleton Island! Cap'n Flint killed him and put him here - as a compass.'

Morgan said, 'It's Allardyce. He took my knife with him. I remember now.'

'Well, the knife isn't here now. Where is it?' asked George.

'Maybe Flint took it,' Morgan said. 'Maybe he's still alive!'

'No, he's dead,' said George.

'Well, maybe it's his ghost!' Morgan cried.

'Stop this talk!' shouted Silver. 'Flint is dead and there isn't a ghost. Come, let's go.'

So we continued walking. On the plateau we sat down to rest. We could see the Cape of the Woods in front of us. Behind us was the harbour and Skeleton Island. Above us was Spy-glass hill.

'There are only three tall trees in the direction of Skeleton Island,' Silver said. 'It will be easy now. Come on boys, let's go!'

But suddenly a voice began to sing:

Fifteen men on The Dead Man's Chest - Yo-ho-ho, and a bottle of rum!

It was a strange, high voice, and it came from the trees. The men's faces went white. They stood up quickly.

'Oh God, it's Flint!' said George.

The voice stopped. Silver's face was very white too. But he said, 'Come on, boys, don't be frightened! Someone is playing a game with us.'

The voice suddenly began again. It didn't sing this time.

'Darby M'Graw!' it shouted, from far away. 'Darby M'Graw! Bring the rum. Darby!'

The buccaneers didn't move; they didn't speak.

'I know those words,' Morgan said. 'They were Flint's last words!'

Silver was very frightened too. He said quietly: 'Who knows the name Darby M'Graw on this island? Only us, Flint's men.' Then he said in a loud voice, 'Mates, I want that treasure and nobody will stop me. It is very near here and I'm going to find it!'

'It's Flint's ghost, John!' said Morgan.

'Ghost? Well, that voice had an echo and a ghost's voice doesn't have an echo - am I right, mates?'

'Yes, that's true,' George Merry said. 'You're an intelligent man,

John. Courage, mates! I'm not sure that the voice was Flint's. It was... it was like...'

'Ben Gunn's voice, by God!' shouted Silver.

'Who is frightened of Ben Gunn?'

Merry asked. 'Not me!'

The buccaneers weren't frightened now, and the colour returned to their faces. They began to laugh and talk. Then we continued walking and we arrived at the first of the tall trees. But it wasn't the right one. We went to the second tree; it wasn't Flint's. But the third tree was very tall, about two hundred feet high. We all knew that in the ground under that tree was the treasure!

My companions ran towards it and Silver followed them on his crutch. Sometimes he pulled me with the rope; sometimes he looked at me with terrible eyes that said, 'I'm going to put the treasure on the Hispaniola, and then I'm going to kill you and all your friends,'

Suddenly the men stopped. There was a cry of surprise. In front of us was a very big hole in the ground. It wasn't recent because there was grass in it. There were some pieces of wood with 'Walrus' on them - the name of Flint's ship. But there wasn't any treasure in the hole. It was empty.

The buccaneers couldn't believe their eyes. They just stood and looked at the hole. But John Silver s surprise passed quickly. He said to me quietly:

'Are you ready, Jim?' And he gave me a pistol.

Then quietly he began to move to one side of the hole. Now it was between us and the buccaneers. He looked at me and smiled. The others jumped into the hole and tried to dig with their fingers. Morgan found a piece of money and gave it to his companions.

'Two pounds!' Merry shouted at Silver. 'You knew that the hole was empty!'

'Do you want to be Cap'n, Merry?' Silver answered.

But this time all the pirates were with Merry. And they were all very angry. They began to climb out of the hole. Then we all stood there: two on one side of the hole, five on the other. Silver watched them with a calm expression. Nobody spoke. Then Merry said:

'Mates, there are only two of them. Silver has got one leg and Hawkins is only a boy. Now, mates -'

But he didn't finish. There were three shots from the trees - crack! crack! crack! - and Merry fell dead into the hole. Another pirate fell dead too. The other three ran away. Just then the doctor, Gray and Ben Gunn came out of the trees with their guns.

'Quick, boys!' shouted the doctor. 'To the boats! Before the pirates get there!'

And we all ran into the trees. Silver ran very fast on his crutch. Then he shouted:

'It's all right, doctor! Look, they aren't going to the boats!' So we all sat down to rest.

Soon we went down the hill towards the boats. And Ben Gunn told us his story.

'I found the skeleton of Allardyce a long time ago, and I took his knife. And then two months ago I found the treasure. I took it to a cave in a hill on the north-east of the island. It's there now.'

Then the doctor told us his story.

'When I left the stockade, I went to find Ben Gunn,' he said, 'and he told me his story. Well, the next morning I saw that the ship wasn't there. So I went to Silver and gave him the map because now I knew that it didn't show where the treasure was. Then the squire, the captain and I went to Ben's cave. I didn't want to leave you with the pirates, Jim, but you ran away so what could I do? Then I saw you at the stockade and you told me your story. I knew that your situation was very dangerous, so I ran back to the cave. Gray, Ben and I took our guns. We wanted to arrive at the big tree before you and the pirates.

But you were a long way in front of us. So Ben tried to stop the pirates. He shouted in Captain Flint's voice and the pirates stopped. So we arrived at the tree first and we waited for you.'

When we found the boats, the doctor destroyed one of them and we all got into the other. Then we went towards North Inlet. We passed Ben Gunn's hill and saw his cave. We continued for three miles, and then we suddenly saw the Hispaniola! She wasn't on the beach in North Inlet.

'The sea came in and carried her away,' the doctor said. 'But she's all right. Gray, you can stay on her tonight and guard her.'

So we got out of the boat on the beach at Rum Bay, near Ben's cave, and Gray went to the Hispaniola. When we arrived at the cave the squire met us.

'John Silver,' he said. 'You're a very bad man. But the doctor told me that we mustn't arrest you. You're a lucky man, Silver.'

'Thank you very much, sir,' said Long John.

'Don't thank me, my man! I wanted to arrest you!'

We went into the cave. Captain Smollett was near a big fire. And then I saw Flint's treasure in a corner - lots and lots of gold!

For dinner that night we had Ben's goat and some wine from the Hispaniola. We were all very happy. And Silver sat with us. He talked and laughed.

Early next morning, we took all the treasure to the beach. Then Gray and Ben Gunn took it by boat to the Hispaniola. There was lots of it and we worked all day for three days.

On the third night the doctor and I walked on the hill. We heard some voices far away in the night.

'It's the three pirates,' said the doctor.

'They're all drunk, sir,' said John Silver behind us.

The doctor didn't answer and he didn't look at Silver. The buccaneer was always polite to us now and he always tried to do a lot of things for us. But nobody liked him.

We didn't hear the pirates again and we decided to leave them on the island. We left some food for them. Then we went to the Hispaniola and sailed her away. The three pirates watched us from the island.

'Don't leave us here!' they shouted.

But we didn't take them. They were dangerous and we didn't want any problems. Soon the island was far away; and then there was only the sea. I was very happy.

With only six men we couldn't sail the ship to England, so we went to a port in Spanish America. Lots of Indians came to our ship to sell fruit and vegetables. That night we went to the town and we met an English captain. He took us to his ship for dinner and it was very late when we arrived back on the Hispaniola. Ben Gunn was on board.

He told us that John Silver wasn't there. 'He went away in a boat a few hours ago,' he said. 'I'm sorry. You see, I helped him. But I did it to save your lives. I'm sure he wanted to kill you all. He took some of the treasure with him - about 500 pounds.'

'Well,' said the captain with a smile. 'I think that's cheap. Only 500 pounds and we won't see Silver again!'

I'll finish my story quickly. We found some seamen and sailed to England. When the Hispaniola arrived at Bristol, we divided the treasure between us. Now Captain Smollett doesn't work. Gray saved his money and now he has his own business. Ben Gunn got 1000 pounds and he lost it in three weeks!

I don't know where John Silver is now. Perhaps he's living happily with his parrot Captain Flint. Sometimes I dream about Silver and Treasure Island. Then I wake up suddenly with the voice of Captain Flint in my ears: 'Pieces of eight! Pieces of eight!'

I also thought about poor Jim Hawkins. Where was he? An hour later, somebody called from the woods behind the stockade.

'Doctor! Squire! Captain! Hallo, Hunter, is that you?'

I ran to the door of the cabin. It was Jim Hawkins. He was safe!

Made in the USA
Las Vegas, NV
16 March 2021